The Story Of The

Zebracorn

Gary Anthony

DEDICATION

For Chilou and Cheri, sharing with all who believe

in the power of love and positive thinking.

ACKNOWLEDGMENTS

This book, along with "The Zebracorn Song" sound recording and video,

were adapted from a poem written more than three decades ago.

The words of that poem penned by my friend Tammy Jones and myself,

eventually produced the character presented in this book.

He has survived the test of time.

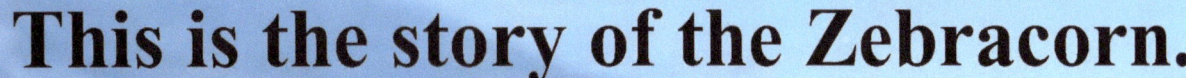

This is the story of the Zebracorn.

...and some people scorn.

It doesn't matter anyhow you see,

'cause what's in our heart will be free.

Lots of people talk about it everyday...

...giving any excuse in many ways.

It's simple, they say...

...that it's just not right.

But wait, just hold on tight.

This is the story...

...of the Zebracorn...

...he's been in hiding you see.

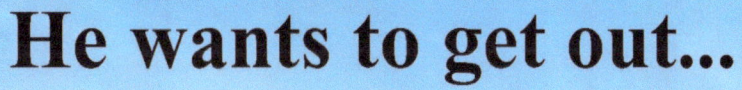

He wants to get out...

...and he's trying to break free.

This is the way it should be.

Now he broke loose...

...things won't be the same.

He's hot to trot,
wants to push it to the limit.

But he knows,
some people just won't give it.

He's a little different...

...but has room to grow.

Let's step aside and...

...just watch him go.

Not ahead of his time,
keeping up with the rest.

Maybe someday,
his way will be the best.

This is the story of the Zebracorn.
It doesn't matter you see...

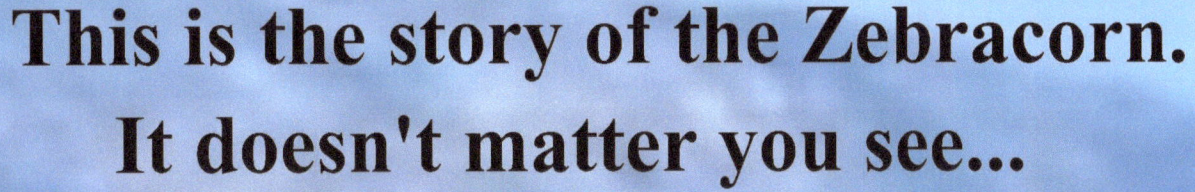

...he may be just a little Zebracorn,
but what's in his heart will be free.